Names for Snow

Judi K. Beach

pictures by

Loretta Krupinski

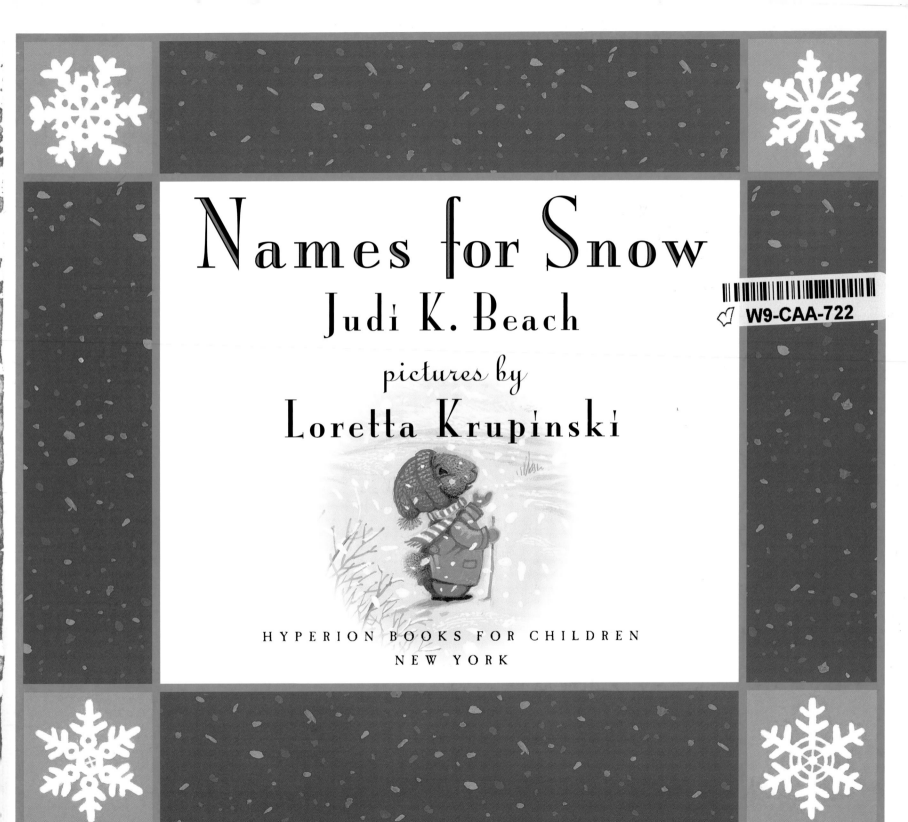

HYPERION BOOKS FOR CHILDREN
NEW YORK

AUTHOR'S NOTE

I've always been fascinated with the art and culture of the Inuits, who live much of their lives with winter weather. In fact, it is said they have more than fifty names for snow—this, as well as my winters in Maine and memories of my childhood winters in Kentucky and Ohio, inspired me as I wrote *Names for Snow.*—Judi K. Beach

For Stewart, who shared with me the many names for love—J.K.B.

For information address Hyperion Books for Children, 114 Fifth Avenue, New York, New York 10011-5690.
Printed in Singapore
This book was set in Caslon Antique. The artwork was prepared using gouache.

First Edition
1 3 5 7 9 10 8 6 4 2
Library of Congress Cataloging-in-Publication Data on file.
ISBN 0-7868-1937-5
Visit www.hyperionchildrensbooks.com

"Mama, what is snow?"

We call it
Welcome in November.

We call it Sheet
when it stretches across
garden beds.

We call those soft, full flakes
floating down
Wings of White Butterflies.

Call it Kitten when it sleeps
in the crook of a window.

Call snow Lace
when it lines the limbs
of the lilacs—

or Eyelet
when it embroiders spruce.

Call it Mother
when it dusts—

or Magician
when the landscape disappears.

Call it Prayer

in its stillness—

and Harmonica
when it whistles through the trees.

Call it Tickle

when you stand, arms outstretched,

and catch it on your tongue.

Call it Tradition
when it comes on Christmas—

and Trickster
when it appears April First.

In the evening,
when snow delivers us
to the comfort
of hearth fire,

. . .we call it Friend.